Frightful's Daughter
MEETS THE Baron Weasel

by JEAN CRAIGHEAD GEORGE

illustrated by DANIEL SAN SOUCI

DUTTON CHILDREN'S BOOKS

DUTTON CHILDREN'S BOOKS
A division of Penguin Young Readers Group
Published by the Penguin Group
Penguin Group (USA) Inc., 375 Hudson Street, New York, New York 10014, U.S.A.
Penguin Group (Canada), 90 Eglinton Avenue East, Suite 700, Toronto, Ontario, Canada M4P 2Y3
(a division of Pearson Penguin Canada Inc.) • Penguin Books Ltd, 80 Strand, London WC2R 0RL,
England • Penguin Ireland, 25 St Stephen's Green, Dublin 2, Ireland (a division of Penguin Books Ltd)
Penguin Group (Australia), 250 Camberwell Road, Camberwell, Victoria 3124, Australia (a division of
Pearson Australia Group Pty Ltd) • Penguin Books India Pvt Ltd, 11 Community Centre, Panchsheel
Park, New Delhi - 110 017, India • Penguin Group (NZ), 67 Apollo Drive, Mairangi Bay, Auckland
1311, New Zealand (a division of Pearson New Zealand Ltd) • Penguin Books (South Africa) (Pty)
Ltd, 24 Sturdee Avenue, Rosebank, Johannesburg 2196, South Africa
Penguin Books Ltd, Registered Offices: 80 Strand, London WC2R 0RL, England

CIP Data is available.

Published in the United States by Dutton Children's Books,
a division of Penguin Young Readers Group
345 Hudson Street, New York, New York 10014
www.penguin.com/youngreaders

Designed by IRENE VANDERVOORT

Printed in China
First Edition
ISBN 978-0-525-47202-5
10 9 8 7 6 5 4 3 2 1

for AiLi George
J.C.G.

In memory of my dear friend Steve Medley—
publisher of the Yosemite Association—
who created so many wonderful nature books
D.S.S.

OKSI, the daughter of Frightful, the legendary peregrine
falcon of the Catskills, was busy hunting to feed her two babies.
Spring was turning to summer. The young birds, called eyases,
were four weeks old, but still not old enough to fly.

Oksi and her eyases were cozied in the nest box erected by Sam Gribley, a boy who lived in the forest on a mountain. Sam's home was the roomy hollow inside an enormous hemlock tree nearby. His friends were the wild birds and beasts that came to visit him. Oksi was his favorite.

Another friend was the Baron Weasel. He was not as sweet and noble as Oksi, but he was dazzling. He could catch rabbits, squirrels, and birds three times his size. He could snag mice and snakes in a lightning flash. Sam admired these traits, but he really liked the Baron Weasel because he was funny. The Baron would suddenly pop up at Sam's feet to say "Boo!" in his weasel way. He would leap in the air and turn twists. He would leave frogs on Sam's bed in the night.

On this June day, however, the Baron was not being funny. He was deadly serious. He was watching Oksi feed her babies on the porch of the nest box—right out in plain view. Baby birds are a weasel delicacy.

The Baron was about to leap from the boulder to the nest box when Falco, Oksi's mate, saw him. He warned *"Rehk! Rehk!* Danger!" and dove. The Baron jumped into the May apples that covered the forest floor. He ducked under their umbrella-like leaves and slipped away. Falco struck the flowers, not him. The Baron's eyes twinkled.

To the Baron a pair of peregrine falcons nesting in a forest was a mistake of nature. Peregrine falcons nest on cliffs and sometimes even city buildings with endless vistas, not in forests. But Oksi did things her own way. She had grown up in the nest box after Sam rescued her from falcon thieves. And to Sam's nest box she had returned in spring to lay her eggs.

Sam Gribley did not really think the Baron could leap as high as the nest box, but he measured it once more to make sure. The pole was almost fourteen feet tall. No weasel could jump that high. And Sam thought no weasel could climb that pole. He had polished it as smooth as the inside of a clam.

Sam was very protective of Oksi. When he saw the Baron creeping back toward her nursery, he shook his fist. "None of that, Baron!" he shouted. "Stay away from the babies." The Baron scurried off.

Satisfied that Oksi's little eyases were safe, Sam went to catch a fish for supper.

Off to his den the Baron Weasel ran, down a long tunnel carpeted with mouse fur. It looped around a boulder, wove between hemlock roots, and ended at the weasel nursery. The four baby weasels there were screeching with hunger. The Baroness was out hunting, and since both weasel parents feed the young, the Baron slipped out to get a mouse from the pantry. It was empty. The Baron needed to feed his babies soon. He turned a back somersault in the narrow space, flipped over, and sped down a third tunnel. He emerged not far from the nest-box pole.

All was quiet. Without blinking an eye, the Baron Weasel climbed right up the pole as if it were a weasel staircase.

When he was halfway to the nest box, a bullet of feathers sped at him.

The Baron let go, dropped into the May apple leaves, then stood up on his hind legs. His eyes twinkled. The Baron Weasel had met Oksi, and Oksi had met the Baron Weasel. She knew what to do: get her babies on their wings immediately and take them far away.

The Baron was disappointed, but he would try again. His babies were still hungry. He needed to distract Oksi while he climbed to her nest.

Just after sunup the Baron followed his nose to a dead pheasant Sam had stored in his springhouse. But he did not get a bite. Sam's raccoon friend, Jesse Coon James, was already there, finishing a last morsel. A red fox sat nearby, licking her paw as if to say "That was good." All that remained of the bird were two large feathered wings. Then the Baron came up with a clever plan. He grabbed a wing tightly in his teeth, flipped it onto his back, and ran out into the dawn.

Oksi saw the pheasant wing jerking across the forest floor. Food! She dove. The Baron heard the wind sing through her feathers. He dropped the prize and slid away. Oksi struck the wing one powerful blow and looked at it. Something was wrong. It did not flutter. She carried it to the foot of a nearby tree and pecked at it.

While she was occupied, the Baron Weasel dashed to the pole and climbed to the bottom of the nest box.

There he was stumped. He could not walk upside down on the underside of the porch to reach the eyases. But he saw a knothole in the porch floor. Small as it was, the knothole was an open doorway for a limber, slender weasel. He stretched out and poked his nose through the hole. Before he could pull himself up, Oksi was diving at him.

The Baron hit the ground and ran. His eyes twinkled.

The next day, Oksi and Falco watched the eyases flap their wings without flying. Oksi urged them to take off by holding food in her talons and calling to them softly. They would not even try. Oksi and Falco flew off to hunt.

The little falcons were left alone. The Baron saw his opportunity. He kangarooed over the leaves and climbed the pole to the nest box. He poked his head through the knothole—but his shoulders were too big to follow. Above the eyases he saw a limb of Sam's ancient hemlock tree.

The eyases looked at the Baron's bright eyes and screamed. Oksi heard their cry and called *"Rehk, rehk, rehk!"* The blue jays heard Oksi's alarm and added, *"Yek, yek, yek!"* to the din. The crows heard the jays and flew, cawing and yelling, to the hemlock tree as Sam looked up from the pond and saw the Baron Weasel coming down the hemlock limb toward the eyases.

"No, you don't!" he shouted.

Jays dove, crows yelled, and the Baron dropped into the leaves and disappeared. Sam grabbed a handful of clay from the pond edge, shinnied up the pole, and plugged up the knothole.

"Wow," he said as he slid back to earth, "peace is sure hard to come by."

Days passed. Oksi and Falco tried to make their eyases fly by flying at them. They would not. The parents brought food to them and taunted them with it as they tried to make them fly. They would not.

The Baron Weasel loped off to Sam's acorn-and-nut pantry and caught all the mice and rats.

Sam's world was now peaceful. The Baron was doing what good weasels do, catching mice and rats. Oksi and Falco were doing what good falcon parents do, feeding their young. And the eyases were doing what six-week-old eyases do—flapping their wings and getting ready to fly. But still they wouldn't. Life was much too comfortable in the nest box.

The Baron Weasel, however, had not forgotten about the little falcons.

One day Sam went off to gather wild strawberries. Oksi and Falco went hunting. No sooner had they departed than the hemlock limb above the nest box began to dance. It dipped and bounced. The curious eyases sat back on their heels and stared at it.

Suddenly, out of the greenery sailed the Baron Weasel. He glided over the heads of the little falcons and landed with a soft thud on the top of the nest box, then leaped to the floor.

The eyases jumped in fright, flapped their wings—and flew.

Out in the meadow, Sam saw the young falcons flying over-
head. They were headed for the river and its cliffs, where peregrine falcons belong.

"Good-bye," Sam called as they soared away. "It was great to
have you. Oh, and tell Oksi to come back next year."

Sam was on his way home when the Baron Weasel popped up suddenly in the middle of the path to say "Boo!" in his weasel way.

"Yikes," Sam said, and laughed. "You scared me. Which reminds me, thanks for ending your jump-and-scare game with the baby falcons. And while I'm at it, thanks for ridding my pantry of mice. You're really a very sweet guy, Baron Weasel."

The Baron's eyes shone brightly.

The Baron arched his back and ran off. Four little weasels, their eyes glistening, got in line behind him to learn the weasel role in the eternal life of the forest.